TROT TROT to BOSTON

PLAY RHYMES FOR BABY

Compiled By Carol F. Ra
Pictures by Catherine Stock

Lothrop, Lee & Shepard Books
New York

First Edition 1 2 3 4 5 6 7 8 9 10
Library of Congress Cataloging in Publication Data
Ra, Carol F. Trot, trot to Boston. Summary: A collection of traditional nursery play rhymes with instructions for accompanying activities. Bibliography: p. 1. Nursery rhymes. 2. Children's poetry. [1. Nursery rhymes. 2. Finger plays] I. Stock, Catherine, ill. II. Title. PZ7.3.R114Tr 1987 398′.8 86-7354 ISBN 0-688-06190-7 ISBN 0-688-06191-5 (lib. bdg.)
Printed in Hong Kong.

For my parents, Samuel and Elsie Hawn,
who taught me the best things I know —C.F.R.

For Fiona and Sean —C.S.

Trot, trot to Boston,
To buy a loaf of bread.
Trot, trot home again,
The old trot's dead.

*Your baby will love horse rides on your foot or knee. Simply bounce
gently. When you pretend to be tired at the end of this rhyme, your
baby will be delighted but will soon spur you back to Boston!*

Catch her, crow!
Carry her, kite!
Take her away till the
    apples are ripe.
When they are ripe and
    ready to fall—
Here comes baby,
Apples and all!

Your leg can be baby's first sliding board. The slide from your knee to your foot at the end of this rhyme is baby's favorite part. Let your baby's expression guide the speed of the ride.

Here we go
down–down–down.

Here we go
up–up–up.

Here we go
backward and forward.

And here we
go round–round–round.

Baby will enjoy the variety of movements while riding on the foot of your crossed leg. Your baby will soon learn the meaning of each motion word since it is associated with the anticipation of the new action.

Babies love the wonderful galloping rhythm of this rhyme. When you say it, emphasize the appropriate words in order to give it its gallop, as in: "To market, to market, to buy a fat pig." This delightful movement will help your child internalize a sense of rhythm.

To market, to market,
To buy a fat pig,
Home again, home again,
Jiggety jig.
To market, to market,
To buy a fat hog,
Home again, home again,
Jiggety jog.
To market, to market,
To buy a plum bun,
Home again, home again,
Market is done.

Much fun comes as each child rides for the first time to this old market. With repetition, a baby who knows only a few words may surprise you by being able to fill in the second word in a pair of rhyming words, especially if you strongly emphasize the first.

Leg over leg,
  as the dog went to Dover,
When he came to a stile,
  JUMP! He went over.

As you lift your baby up from your knee on JUMP!, baby will laugh. But don't move too quickly! The expectation of the jump is nearly as exciting for baby as the jump itself.

Ride away, ride away,
    Johnny shall ride,
And he shall have pussy-cat
    tied to one side;
And he shall have little dog
    tied to the other,
And Johnny shall ride
    to see his grandmother.

Using your baby's name in this rhyme makes the gallop to grand-mother's seem real.

Head bumper,
Eye winker,
Nose dropper,
Mouth eater,
Chin chopper,
Gully, gully, gully!

Babies enjoy face rhymes. They like the building anticipation caused by starting at the top of the head and working downward to the chin. The little tickle under the chin at the end of most face rhymes is meant to be gentle, not intrusive. In time, your baby will want to touch your face and tickle under your chin as you say the rhyme.

Here sits the Lord Mayor.
Touch forehead.
Here sit his men.
Point to eyes.
Here sits the cockadoodle.
Right cheek,
Here sits the hen.
Left cheek,
Here sit the little chickens,
Nose,
Here they run in.
Mouth.
Chin chopper, chin chopper,
chin chopper, chin.
Tickle chin.

This rhyme is fun at any time, but is especially fitting at baby's mealtime. Food may be offered at the end of the last line, "One little mouth that likes to eat."

Ring the bell.
> *Gentle tug at lock of hair.*

Knock at the door,
> *Tap on forehead.*

Peep in,
> *Peep into eyes.*

Lift the latch,
> *Lift nose.*

Walk in.
> *Point to baby's mouth.*

Go way down to the cellar
> *Walk fingers down chin to throat.*

And eat apples.
> *Little tickle.*

Round and round
the garden
Like a teddy bear.
One step, two steps,
Tickle you
under there!

Draw circles on your baby's palm as you say the first part of this rhyme, then walk your fingers up the arm like a teddy bear lumbering to its underarm den. End this rhyme—and those that follow—with a little tickle under the arm or, if baby prefers, a squeeze of the shoulder. The best part of all the play rhymes is holding your baby on your lap and laughing together.

Round about the rosebush,
Three steps,
Four steps,
All the little boys and girls
Are sitting on the doorstep.

With your finger draw a circle on baby's palm. Then walk two fingers up to the inside of the elbow where you rest your hand and wiggle your fingers upward to represent "all the little boys and girls." Children are fascinated by the many ways in which fingers can dramatize actions in play rhymes. After repetition, your child will want to practice on you.

Here goes a turtle up the hill—
Creepy, creepy, creepy, creepy.
Here goes a rabbit up the hill—
Boing, boing, boing, boing.
Here goes an elephant up the hill—
Thud, thud, thud, thud.
Here goes a snake up the hill—
Slither, slither, slither, slither.
Here comes a rock down the hill—
Boom, boom, boom, boom, CRASH!

Different animals may be used each time the game is played. Starting at your baby's palm, walk each animal (your fingers) up to the top of the shoulder, moving in a characteristic way and making appropriate sounds. Your fist is the rock on top of the hill (baby's shoulder) in the last line. It booms down the hill with all the animals and ends in baby's palm on CRASH! This folk game is played in Malaysia.

Round about there
Sat a little hare.
The bow-wows came
     and chased him
Right up there!

After drawing a circle on baby's palm, run four fingers up the arm to the top of the shoulder. Repeatedly thump the top of the shoulder with the fingers to represent the animals' tumbling together. Baby will wriggle and laugh.

Round about, round about,
Catch a wee mouse.

Up a bit, up a bit,
In a wee house.

Draw the mouse's path on baby's hand. Then scurry two fingers up to the underarm house. Touching under the arm rather than tickling may be preferred by your baby.

Pat-a-cake,
Help baby do motions: Clap hands.

Pat-a-cake,
Clap hands.

Baker's man,
Clap hands.

Bake me a cake
Clap hands.

As fast as you can.
Clap hands.

Roll it,
Roll hands around each other.

And pat it,
Pat one hand on top of the other.

And mark it with "B,"
Draw "B" on baby's palm.

And put it in the oven
Pat baby's tummy.

For baby and me!

Babies love this classic. To make it even more fun, substitute your baby's initial and name for "B" and "baby."

The dog says *bow wow.*
The cow says *moo, moo.*
The lamb says *baa, baa.*
The duck says *quack, quack.*
And the kitty cat says *meee—OW!*

Beginning with the thumb for the dog, each finger of your baby's hand represents one of the animals. On the little finger the cat says "meee-." Then nip the little finger lightly with a pinch as you say "OW!" If you make a funny face as if in pain when you say "OW!" your baby will find it even funnier.

This little cow eats grass.

This little cow eats hay.

This little cow drinks water.

This little cow runs away.

This little cow does nothing, but just lies down all day.
We'll chase her, we'll chase her, we'll chase her away.

With the thumb representing the first little cow, touch each finger in turn. When you get to the last cow (the little finger), tickle it and run your fingers up to the top of baby's shoulder.

Put your finger in
Foxy's hole.
Foxy's not at home.
Foxy's at the back door,
Picking on a bone.

Babies like the mystery of this game. Your fist represents foxy's hole. While saying the first line, show your baby how to put a finger into the top of your fist. On the last line, foxy may mistake baby's finger for a bone—nip the finger gently with your little finger. The mystery comes in not knowing when foxy may nip the finger.

This little piggy went to market.

This little piggy stayed home.

This little piggy had roast beef.

This little piggy had none.

This little piggy went *wee, wee, wee,* All the way home.

This old rhyme is fresh and delightful to each baby. Babies usually love to have their toes touched—start with the big toe for the first little piggy. The real fun is anticipating the "Wee, wee, wee" when the little toe is tweaked and the last piggy runs up to baby's chin—"all the way home."

Shoe the little horse,
Tap the bottom of one bare foot.
Shoe the little mare,
Tap the bottom of the second foot.
With a tap-tap here,
Tap the first foot.
And a tap-tap there,
Tap the second foot.
But let the little colt go *bare*!
Hold the ankles and lift both feet high,
drawing circles.

Play this rhyme when the baby is lying down.

This is baby ready for a nap,
Lift your index finger.
Lay baby down in a loving lap.
Lay your finger in baby's palm.
Cover baby up so it won't peep.
Baby closes fingers around your index finger.
Rock the baby till it's fast asleep.

We all know how babies love to be rocked. The rocking chair offers a welcome transition between playtime and bedtime. Babies relax and feel reassured when rocking in the lap of someone they love.